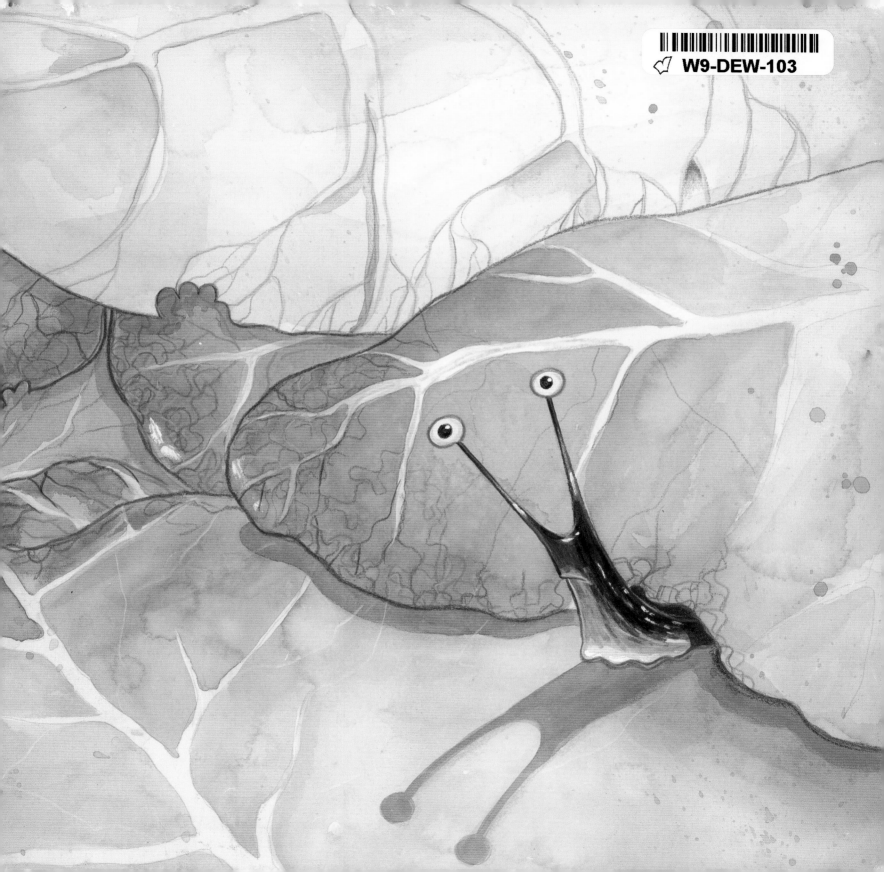

For Kimmy and Copper
~ A P

For Eugene
~ D R

Copyright © 2005 by Good Books, Intercourse, PA 17534
International Standard Book Number: 1-56148-488-1
Library of Congress Catalog Card Number: 2005002672

Original edition published in English by Little Tiger Press,
an imprint of Magi Publications, London, England, 2005.

Printed in Belgium by Proost N.V.

Library of Congress Cataloging-in-Publication Data

Powell, Anna, 1949-
Don't say that, Willy Nilly! / Anna Powell ; illustrated by David Roberts.
p. cm.

Summary: While on his way to the store to buy cabbage for dinner,
Willy Nilly manages to say the wrong thing to almost everyone he meets.
ISBN 1-56148-488-1 (hardcover)
[1. Humorous stories.] I. Title: Do not say that, Willy Nilly.
II. Roberts, David, 1970- ill. III. Title.

PZ7.P87712Don 2005
[E]--dc22

2005002672

Don't Say That, Willy Nilly!

Anna Powell

Illustrated by
David Roberts

Good Books

Intercourse, PA 17534
800/762-7171
www.goodbks.com

"Willy Nilly," said his mother,
"would you like to go to the store
and buy some cabbage for dinner?"
"YUK!" said Willy Nilly.

"Don't say that, Willy Nilly," said his mother. "Say, 'YUM, YUM, WHAT A LOVELY DINNER!'"

"Yum, yum, what a lovely dinner?" repeated Willy Nilly.

"That's right," said his mother.

"GOT IT!" said Willy Nilly.

So Willy Nilly set off to the store.

"YUM, YUM, **WHAT A LOVELY DINNER!**
YUM, YUM, **WHAT A LOVELY DINNER!**"
repeated Willy Nilly.

Outside, the men were emptying garbage cans.
Willy Nilly said, "Yum, yum,
what a lovely dinner!"

"Don't say that, Willy Nilly," said the garbage men. "Say, 'GOOD RIDDANCE TO BAD GARBAGE!'"

"Good riddance to bad garbage?" said Willy Nilly. "That's right," said the men.

"GOT IT!" said Willy Nilly.

"GOOD RIDDANCE TO BAD GARBAGE! GOOD RIDDANCE TO BAD GARBAGE!"

In the road there was a big moving truck.

The neighbors were moving away.

Willy Nilly said, "Good riddance to bad garbage!"

"Don't say that, Willy Nilly," said Mrs. Jiggs. "Say, 'ENJOY YOUR NEW HOME!'"

"Enjoy your new home?" said Willy Nilly.

"That's right," said Mrs. Jiggs.

"GOT IT!" said Willy Nilly.

"ENJOY YOUR NEW HOME!
ENJOY YOUR NEW HOME!"
said Willy Nilly as he crossed the park.

The park-keeper was removing some litter
from the pond. He began to wobble and . . .

...fell into the water with a big

SPLASH!

"Enjoy your new home," said Willy Nilly.
"Don't say that, Willy Nilly," said the
park-keeper. "Say, 'CAN I HELP YOU OUT OF THERE?'"
"Can I help you out of there?" said Willy Nilly.
"That's right," said the park-keeper.
"GOT IT!" said Willy Nilly.

Mr. Totty's window was open. The parrot
looked at Willy Nilly with a beady yellow eye.
"Can I help you out of there?" said Willy Nilly.
"WATCH OUT, I MIGHT BITE!" said the parrot.

"Watch out, I might bite!"
said Willy Nilly.
   "WATCH OUT, I MIGHT BITE!"
said the parrot.
   "GOT IT!" said Willy Nilly.

"WATCH OUT, I MIGHT BITE!
WATCH OUT, I MIGHT BITE!"

On the pavement Willy met Granny Macaroon.
"Good morning, Willy Nilly!" said Granny Macaroon.
"Watch out, I might bite!" said Willy Nilly.

"Don't say that, Willy Nilly,"
said Granny Macaroon. "Say,
'WHAT A LOVELY DAY!'"
   "What a lovely day?"
said Willy Nilly.
   "That's right," said
Granny Macaroon.
   "GOT IT!" said Willy Nilly.

"WHAT A LOVELY DAY!
WHAT A LOVELY DAY!"

The window cleaner sped past on his bicycle.
He wasn't looking where he was going.
He was heading straight for the lamppost.

"What a lovely day!" said Willy Nilly.

CRASH!

"Don't say that, Willy Nilly!"
said the window cleaner. "Say,
'HEY, LOOK OUT!'"
    "Hey, look out!" repeated Willy Nilly.
    "That's right," said the window cleaner.
    "GOT IT!" said Willy Nilly.

In the store, there was a baby in a stroller. Willy Nilly saw the baby reach out to a tower of cans. Oh no! The cans would fall on top of him. **"HEY, LOOK OUT!"** shouted Willy Nilly.

And the baby stopped! Just in time. "Quick thinking, young man," said the storekeeper. "What can I do for you?"

"A cabbage, please," said Willy Nilly.
"And what would you like as a
thank you?" said the storekeeper.
Willy Nilly chose his favorite
thing – ketchup. "Thank you very
much," he said.

Willy Nilly went straight home.
"Did you get the cabbage, Willy Nilly?"
asked his mother.
"GOT IT!" said Willy Nilly.
"Thank you very much,"
said his mother, and
she cooked the cabbage.

Willy Nilly poured ketchup all over his cabbage to make it taste nice.

"YUM, YUM, WHAT A LOVELY DINNER!" said Willy Nilly.

"YUK!" said his mother.

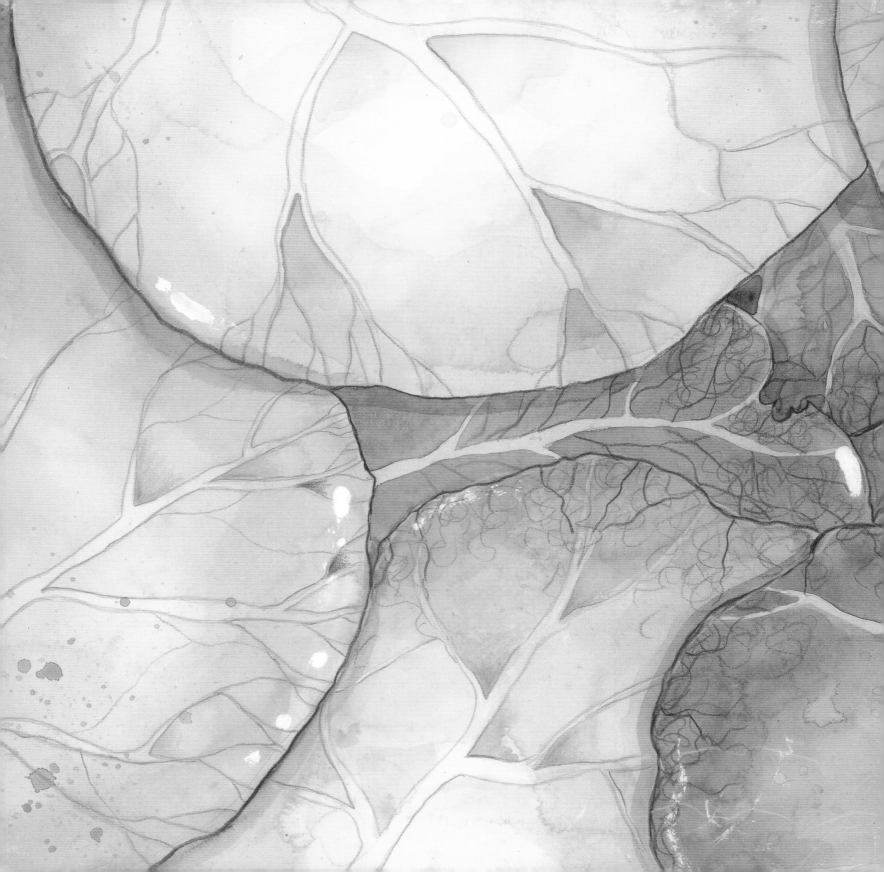